thank YOU!

Hi, Lily!
I hope you
enjoy reading
"Opal."

This book belongs to

Lily

# Opal

Kendra Leah Desai

Even though Opal is a bird, she isn't very good at flying.
Since Opal spends so much of her time walking,
she always wears her pink tennis shoes.

She is on her way to the antique shop
to look for decorative eggs.

"Hi, Mr. Carmel! Do you have any new eggs?" Opal asks eagerly.
"Well, hello Miss Opal. I just got a shipment,
unlike any I've ever seen!"

Opal is so excited!
She chooses her two favorite eggs
        and heads home with a pep in her step.

She is very happy!

On the way, a mean grasshopper named Aiden stops her
and begins to brag that he can jump higher than she can fly.

It hurts her feelings, but she tries to act
as if it doesn't bother her and keeps walking.

She doesn't want Aiden
to ruin her great mood.

She may not be able to fly, but she's good at so many other things. In fact, Opal won a cooking contest last year. She has the best worm and dumpling stew in town. All the local birds love it, especially Emerson the woodpecker. Opal always admired him, so she was very excited when he loved her stew.

Emerson likes to thump his beak on tree trunks.
It's like music to Opal's ears.

Thump, da dun
gada da dum,
gada da dump
thump da dun
da dum!

"Hi Emerson!" "What are you up to?"
"I'm building a new house. I've almost finished the living room.
Come up and see." Opal felt embarrassed, she wasn't sure she could
fly all the way up to his house.

"Um, I don't have time
today. Maybe tomorrow."

She rushes home, upset that she isn't able to tell Emerson the truth. She is in such a hurry that she runs right into Aiden.

"Hey, watch where you're going chubby," he shouts.

"I'm not chubby, I'm just fluffy!" she exclaims.

Her wonderful day is becoming rather crummy.

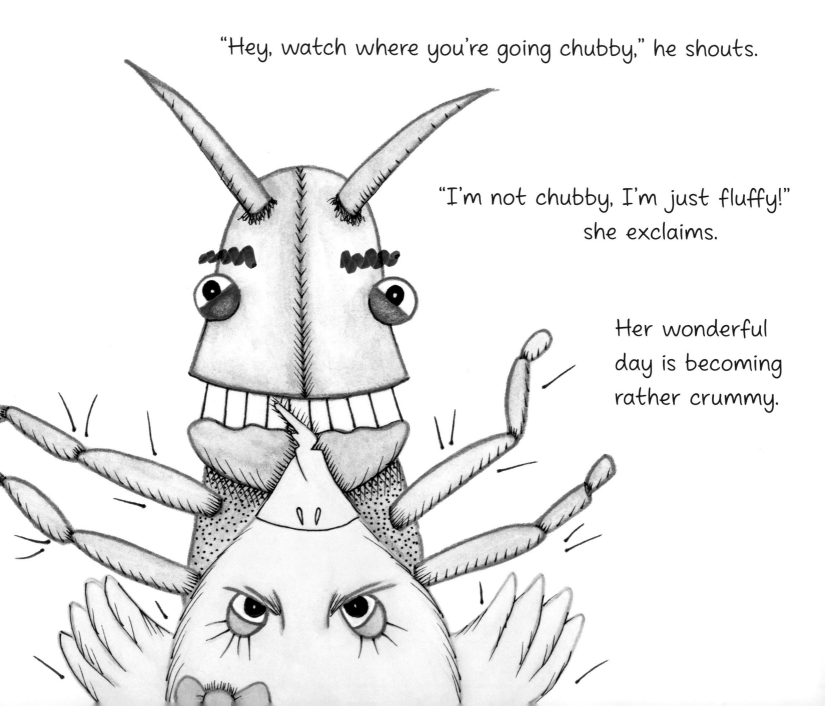

Opal unwraps the new additions to her egg collection as her upset feelings begin to fade.

She is happiest among her collection.

She calls Emerson and invites him over.

"I love your worm and dumpling stew! Of course I'll come to dinner. See you tonight!"

Opal goes to her yard and
finds the plumpest, juiciest
worms for her stew.

She skips back inside,
whistling a happy tune.

The stew is coming along nicely, and the whole house begins to smell of yummy dumpling goodness. The table is set and Emerson will be arriving soon. Time to get ready.

Opal puts on her favorite ruffled socks
and squirts on some perfume.

Just as she is finishing up, she hears
a knock on the door.

Emerson greets her with a tree branch that has been carved into a flower. She adores it!

"Thanks for having me over, Opal."

Opal places the flower in front of her favorite egg.

"These are incredible! I didn't know you were a collector.
I collect antique carving tools. You should come see them
when I finish my tree house."

Opal didn't want to talk about flying up to his place yet, so she quickly rushes to the kitchen...

"Let's eat before
                the stew gets cold!"

It is obvious from Emerson's smile that he really enjoys the stew. Opal is sad when the evening comes to an end, but she is also glad that flying up to his tree house didn't come up again.

Opal decides to go into
the woods to practice flying.

"Maybe I just need to
try harder," she thinks.

She tries, again and again. Something is keeping her from
flying higher. What is it? She realizes that every time she
gets higher her heart begins to beat faster. She lands on
the ground one last time and begins to cry.

How can this be possible?
Birds are not supposed to be afraid of heights.

Opal is not very pleased with herself and runs back home. Along the way, she sees mean Aiden again.

"It's the fluffy fowl that doesn't fly! Ha ha!"

Opal thinks to herself, "Aiden just wants to upset me and I'm not going to let him. Besides, I'm already frustrated with myself. Ignore him, ignore him, ignore him!"

Opal calls her friend Connie, and tells her about her fear of heights. Connie encourages her to tell Emerson, too. He's a true friend, so he should understand.
Opal knows that Connie is right.

Opal walks over to Emerson's and shouts up at him.
"Hey Emerson, would you mind coming down here?"
"Not at all, be right there." Opal waits, nervously,
but knows she is about to do the right thing.

"Hi, what's going on?" asked Emerson.

"I wanted to talk to you about flying up to your house. I'm really afraid of heights and don't know if I'll be able to make it."

"Nonsense", says Emerson, "you're a bird! It's easy, I'll help you!"

"Start flying and I'll support you. Don't worry, if you start to fall, I'll catch you. You can trust me." She begins to flap her wings and sure enough she is able to get up to the house on the first try. She was really scared the entire time, but it felt nice to have his support.

"See, you did it!"
Emerson cheerfully exclaimed.

"I just finished hanging my antique tool collection."

Emerson gives Opal a tour of his new home. He points out every detail of craftsmanship. She can see that he is very talented.

"It's getting late. I better get going. Will you please help me fly back down? This is the scariest part for me."

"Of course, you can always count on me for help."

Emerson helps Opal down and gives her a big hug.
"Thanks for helping me fly," she says with a smile.

"I have lots of stew left, maybe you
can come by for lunch tomorrow?"

"I'd love that, see you then."

On the way home, Opal practices flying.
Thanks to Emerson, her fear is starting to go away.
What a wonderful friend, she thinks to herself.

Things are looking up!

Library of Congress Cataloging-in-Publication Data Available

2 0 1 4 9 1 3 7 1 6

Text and Illustrations © Kendra Leah Desai 2014

Published in Santa Monica, California

ISBN: 978-0-9916613-0-5

Dear Grandmommie,

I know that it was you who
brought Opal to me in a dream.
I dedicate this to you and I thank
you for always being there for me.
May your beautiful spirit continue
to fly. I love you more than words
could ever explain and I miss you
every day.

Love,

Kendra